# THE BROTHER NOBODY KEPT

DURGAM AJAY

To the sisters I begged the universe for...
And the boy I became trying to keep them.

To Keerthi your silence still screams inside me.
To Aishu—you left when I needed you the most.
To Nisha—you forgot me like I was a phase.
To Chinni—you misunderstood my care as something else.
To Divya—you broke a heart that had already shattered too many times.

I called you sister.
Not because it sounded sweet...
But because that word was the only way I knew how to love—without asking
for anything in return.

I was the boy who remembered every birthday.
Who stayed up just to see if you were okay.
Who smiled through pain, just so you wouldn't feel guilty.

This book is not a story. It's a graveyard of every bond I buried while pretending
to be okay.

If you ever wonder what happened to that boy who cared too much—
He's here.

In these pages.
In every line.

Still loving.
Still breaking.

Still the brother nobody kept.

# Contents

# Foreword

This is not just a story.
It's a collection of scars that never fully healed.
Of names that once meant everything
and now live only in memory.
I didn't write this book to be understood.
I wrote it because I needed to breathe.
Because holding it all in was killing me—
quietly, slowly, painfully.
Every chapter in these pages is a grave I've stood beside.
Of bonds buried alive.
Of sisters I never had by blood,
but loved harder than anyone ever knew.
If you've ever trusted someone with your soul,
called them family,
and watched them walk away like you were nothing—
this story is yours too
Because in a world full of people who forget too quickly,
I chose to remember.
And in remembering,
I found something worth sharing.
So here it is—
the ache I lived with,
the truth I couldn't say out loud,
and the love that stayed,
even when no one else did.
— Kanna

# Preface

I never imagined that the word "Anna" would carry so much weight. That one word could hold a world of love, loyalty, pain, and heartbreak.

But it did. For me, it still does.

This book was born from silence—
from the messages I never sent,
the calls that went unanswered,
and the moments I replayed in my head a thousand times, wondering,
"What did I do wrong?"

It's strange, isn't it?
How people can walk into your life, make you feel like you finally belong,
and then leave—like they were never there to begin with.

I didn't write this story to blame anyone.
I wrote it because my heart needed a place to bleed.

Each chapter you're about to read is a mirror of the boy I was, the pain I carried,
and the love I gave—even when there was no one left to receive it.

You might not know Kanna,
But if you've ever felt forgotten,
if you've ever loved someone who outgrew you,
if you've ever stayed loyal to a bond that broke you—
then maybe you've been Jay too.

This isn't just my story.
It's yours too.

  —Kanna

# Acknowledgements

To everyone who came into my life and called me Anna—
thank you for giving me a reason to smile,
even if you didn't stay long enough to see the tears.

To Keerthi, Aishu, Nisha, Chinni, and Divya—
You may never read this.
You may never know how much you meant to me.
But every word in this book exists because you did.

To my mother—
You raised me with love even when you were broken yourself.
You are the reason I learned how to give, how to care, how to survive.

To the readers—
If you picked up this book,
you've already held a piece of my soul.
Thank you for giving it a home.

To the pain—
Thank you for not destroying me.
For turning me into a writer instead.

And finally—
To the boy inside me who kept loving, even after everyone left...
You're not weak.
You're just rare.

# Prologue

I don't remember the day my father died.

I was only two years old—too young to understand loss, but old enough to carry the absence forever.

They say you can't miss what you never had.

But I did.

I missed a voice I never heard.

A hand I never held.

A love I never knew—but always needed.

And so, I grew up chasing pieces of what I didn't get.

A word here.

A hug there.

A smile that felt like it meant something.

But what I longed for most... was a sister.

And I found it.

Again, and again.

Only to lose it.

Again, and again.

Keerthi. Aishu. Nisha. Chinni. Divya.

They called me Anna—and I believed them like a prayer.

But people are temporary.

Words are fragile.

And promises? They're just soft lies dressed in affection.

Every goodbye left a scar.

Every silence taught me how to scream inside.

And now, as I sit with a heart stitched together by memory and grief,

I write this story—not to be heard,

but to be understood.

Because sometimes, the loudest pain is the one no one notices.

I was never asking for love.

I was only asking for someone to stay.

# The Lonely Beginning

*""Some stories don't start with fireworks or fairytales.*
*Some begin in silence...*
*In an empty cradle, beside a grieving mother."*

2003 – A Cry That Changed Everything

The rain beat steadily against the windows as the clock struck midnight. In the sterile white room of a hospital, the world welcomed a baby boy into its arms. But there was one voice missing among the many—the one voice that should have been there to say, "It's a boy!" His father's voice. That voice never came.

Kanna's father had died when Kanna was just two years old. There was no goodbye. No final words. Just an empty space where a father should have been.

Kanna's first memory wasn't of his father's smile, or the comfort of being held in his arms, but the emptiness of a house that should have been filled with laughter, the absence of footsteps that should have echoed beside him as he grew. Instead, it was only his mother, who held him through every night and every tear, giving him everything she could to make up for the man he would never know.

*""How do you miss someone you've never known?*
*It's strange. But I did. Every single day."*

Kanna's mother, Aarti, became his universe. She was his everything. She was the sun, the moon, and the stars. As he grew, he learned that love wasn't just about the things you could see, but about the sacrifices made in silence. His mother worked tirelessly, sewing clothes for families who never saw her wear a single new piece herself, cooking meals for strangers when her own stomach growled with hunger.

She lived for him. She fought for him. She breathed for him.

But even with all her strength, Kanna couldn't help but feel the weight of the silence. He'd watch other children with their fathers, laughing together, sharing small jokes, running home in the evenings to the sound of a father's voice calling them inside.

But for him, there was no such sound. No father's laughter. No deep voice telling him to be brave, to be strong, to never give up.

Only his mother, who could never fill that void, no matter how hard she tried.

*"She gave me everything... except the one thing life never let her give me—a complete family."*

As a child, Kanna was quiet. His mother always said he was thoughtful, observant—never a troublemaker. He would sit alone for hours, playing with his toys, building worlds with Legos and blocks. He could lose himself in the play, but when it came to the end of the day, the world would come rushing back. The absence. The quiet. The loneliness that crept up on him like the shadows at dusk.

Every birthday, every celebration felt like a reminder. His friends had siblings to fight with, to share moments of joy and tears with, but for Kanna, there was always the empty seat at the dinner table, the unspoken question in his heart: Why don't I have a sister?

*"We are all born into families, but what if the one you are born into isn't complete?"*

He would often find himself lying in bed late at night, staring at the ceiling, imagining what it would be like to have someone beside him. Someone to share his thoughts with. To share his dreams. A sister. Someone who would know his deepest fears, and would never judge him. Someone to hold his hand when life became too much.

Kanna's dreams were simple. *God, give me a sister. I don't need anything else. I don't need a father. But I need someone to call me "Anna." A voice, soft and sweet, calling him by that name, the one he heard from other kids but could never hear for himself.

*"You know what's worse than being alone?*
*Hoping you won't be."*

School started, and Kanna was a model student. His grades were perfect, his manners impeccable. But there was a quiet sadness behind his eyes, something nobody noticed. Teachers would praise him for his diligence, for being the best in class. But they never saw the way his eyes would linger on the children with their siblings, holding hands, laughing together.

Lunchtime was the hardest part. It was when the other kids would sit in groups—some with their siblings, others with friends—and Kanna would sit alone, picking at his food, pretending not to care. He would occasionally glance at the bench where siblings would sit, chatting, sharing food, laughing. He would think to himself, One day, maybe that will be me.

But that day never came.

*"Some children dream of toys, bikes, or candies.*
*I dreamed of a Rakhi tied on my wrist."*

Growing Up in a World of Gaps

As the years went by, the gaps grew larger. Kanna's longing for a sibling became an ache, a constant companion that shadowed every moment of his life. His friends would talk about their brothers and sisters—about the fights, the teasing, the shared secrets. But Kanna had nothing to share. He only had his mom's tired smile, her warm embrace, and the distant sound of laughter that never seemed to reach him.

There were days when he would try to fill the gap, to pretend he had someone. He'd offer to help the girls in his class, share his lunch, offer a shoulder when they were sad, but deep inside, he knew it wasn't the same. He wasn't looking for a friend. He wasn't looking for a classmate.

He was looking for a sister.

*""Sometimes I'd catch myself imagining a world where I wasn't alone. A world where someone called me 'Anna'—and meant it.""*

One night, after a particularly lonely day, Kanna lay in bed staring at the ceiling again. He whispered softly into the darkness, almost as if speaking to the stars, hoping for someone, anyone, to hear.

"God... just give me a sister. Just one. Someone who will love me without conditions. Someone who will choose me, every day, as I am. Just one... please."

But the darkness swallowed his words. No answers came. Only the hum of the fan, the ticking of the clock. The empty silence that seemed to grow louder with each passing day.

"Some prayers go unanswered. Some wishes fade away before they even have a chance to take root."

The Calm Before the Storm

But little did Kanna know, his life was about to change.

Soon, a girl named Keerthi would walk into his life, and for the first time, he would experience the kind of sibling bond he'd always dreamed of. She would become the sister he had always wanted. She would fill that empty space.

But what Kanna didn't know was... she wouldn't stay. And when she left, it would break him in ways he could never have imagined.

*"Not all beginnings are loud.*
*Some start with a whisper...*
*A lonely boy.*
*An unanswered prayer.*
*And a hope that refuses to die."*

# CHAPTER TWO

# The First Sister – Keerthi

*" "Sometimes, the people we need the most don't arrive with grand gestures...
They come softly, like rain on a summer night—unexpected, but healing." "*

It was the first day of 8th class. Kanna had just stepped into the school gate, his books tucked close to his chest, his heart beating the same lonely rhythm it always had. He didn't expect anything to change. Life had taught him not to hope for miracles.

And then he saw her.

She was standing near the classroom door, adjusting the strap of her school bag. Her hair was tied into two neat braids, a pink ribbon dancing in the morning breeze. There was something different about her—not in her looks, but in her presence. Calm. Gentle. A little lost, just like him.

Keerthi was a new student, recently transferred from another town. She looked unsure, nervous even. The teacher assigned her a seat beside Kanna—fate, perhaps, doing what prayers never could.

*" "Some bonds don't need time. They just need a moment." "*

In the beginning, they spoke little. A few shy glances, occasional exchanges of notes, polite greetings. But slowly, walls began to fall. Kanna, who rarely spoke more than necessary, found himself laughing quietly at her silly jokes. And Keerthi, who was initially reserved, started waiting for Kanna during lunch, even sharing her snacks.

She called him "Kanna," not "Kanna anna" yet—but the way she said his name, it felt different. Safe. Soft. Familiar.

Then came the turning point.

One rainy afternoon, Kanna forgot his umbrella. Everyone else had left. The school compound was nearly empty when he stepped out, bracing himself for the cold downpour. Just as he crossed the gate, a small voice called behind him.

"Wait!"

Keerthi stood there, holding her umbrella out to him. She didn't ask. She didn't hesitate. She simply stepped beside him and smiled.

That day, as they walked home under the shared umbrella, something shifted.

*""You don't choose who becomes your sibling by blood.*
*But sometimes, life lets you choose by bond.""*

"Anna" – The Word That Melted Walls

A few weeks later, after Kanna helped her solve a tough math problem, Keerthi turned to him and softly said:

"Thanks, anna."

That word. That one word.

Kanna froze. His heart, for a moment, forgot how to beat. She had no idea what she had done with that single syllable. It was the word he had begged for in silent prayers. The word that had haunted his dreams.

He smiled, but deep inside, he was crying.

That night, he didn't sleep. He just lay there, hand on his chest, repeating the word again and again.

"Anna."

"Anna."

"Anna."

"It wasn't just a word. It was a bandage. A balm. A home."

The Days That Felt Like Forever

From then on, everything changed.

Keerthi wasn't just a classmate anymore. She became a part of his world. She'd wait for him every morning. They shared secrets—silly ones, serious ones. She'd draw small doodles on the corner of his notebooks. He'd carry her bag if it was too heavy. They had inside jokes, shared songs, and sometimes, they'd just sit in silence, comfortable in each other's presence.

For the first time in Kanna's life, he felt like he belonged to someone. Not romantically. Not as a friend. But as a brother. A protector. A person who mattered.

*""She didn't fix everything.*
*But she made the silence feel less lonely.""*

Then came the virus. COVID-19.

Schools shut down. Streets emptied. People were locked inside their homes. Kanna thought it would be temporary—that he'd see Keerthi again in a few weeks. But weeks turned to months. And slowly, their bond started to feel like a fading photograph.

At first, they texted every day. She'd send memes. He'd send voice notes. They even had video calls, sometimes late into the night, talking about silly things—movies, teachers, future dreams.

But then... the replies became slower. The laughter less frequent. The silences between messages grew heavier. Keerthi had changed.

Kanna tried not to overthink it. Maybe her family was strict. Maybe her phone was taken. Maybe she was just overwhelmed. He kept giving excuses—for her, to himself.

But the ache in his chest said otherwise.

*""The worst part of growing distant is pretending it doesn't*
*hurt.""*

One Last Rakhi

Raksha Bandhan came that year in the middle of lockdown. Kanna had never celebrated it before. But this time, he waited. He cleaned his wrist. He stared at his phone.

Keerthi didn't call.

No Rakhi came. No message. Not even a forwarded greeting.

He told himself it was okay. That it didn't matter. But when he stood in front of the mirror that night, his empty wrist felt like a wound.

He tied a thread himself. One he had saved from a school project. And he whispered:

"Happy Raksha Bandhan, Keerthi."

*""Sometimes, the people who teach us love*
*also teach us loss.""*

A Love That Was Never Romantic, But Was Real

People always misunderstood sibling bonds between boys and girls. They assumed something more. But what Kanna had with Keerthi was sacred.

It was not a crush.

It was not a love story.

It was a bond that held his shattered childhood together.

But life has a cruel way of giving and taking.

And Kanna didn't know yet...

...Keerthi's silence wasn't distance.

It was the beginning of goodbye.

*""Not every goodbye comes with a warning.*
*Some arrive silently, with a slowly fading voice.""*

# Aishu – The Light in the Dark

*" "When darkness wraps itself around your soul,*
*God sends someone with a flickering candle.*
*Not to remove the dark...*
*But to remind you—you're not alone in it." "*

October 2020 – The Phone Call That Shattered the World

It was the day after Dussehra. The skies were unusually grey, not with clouds, but with a silence that felt wrong. Kanna was at home, scrolling through old photos of school days—photos of Keerthi's doodles, their classroom selfies, a short video of her playfully yelling at him to stop being "too serious all the time."

And then the call came.

It was from a common friend. His voice was trembling.

"Kanna... did you hear? Keerthi... tried to kill herself last night."

Kanna's heart stopped.

No.

No, no, no.

Not Keerthi.

Not the girl who called him "anna."

His mind raced. He didn't even ask questions. He just stood there, shaking, trying to process a sentence that didn't make sense. His ears were ringing. His vision blurred. His chest felt like it was caving in.

> *"It's terrifying how someone can be so close to you,*
> *yet you never see the storm inside them."*

Hope on a Hospital Bed

She wasn't gone—yet.

Keerthi was admitted to a hospital. The doctors said it was serious but not hopeless. That one sentence kept Kanna breathing.

He called everyone he could. He tried contacting her family, but they were too overwhelmed. He cried into his pillow at night, begging every god he knew to save her.

Days passed. Hope flickered.

And then, a message popped up on his phone:

"Anna... I heard about Keerthi. You okay?"

It was from Aishu—a senior from his school who had once casually called him "bro" in a WhatsApp group months ago. They had chatted briefly in the past, nothing deep. But now, in the middle of Kanna's storm, her message felt like a fragile hand reaching through the fog.

> *"Sometimes, we don't need people who understand us.*
> *We just need someone who stays."*

From that day, Aishu became a constant.

She called every night. She texted every morning. She listened to his sobs, his silences, his screaming breakdowns. She never said, "Move on." She just said, "Let it out."

They talked about Keerthi—about her laughter, her drawings, her dreams of becoming a lawyer. Aishu even messaged Keerthi once, praying she'd reply. She didn't.

Then Aishu did something Kanna never expected.

She contacted Keerthi's cousin, gathered courage, and visited the hospital.

She sent Kanna voice notes from the outside gates.

"She's still breathing, Kanna... Don't give up."

*""True siblings aren't born.*
*They arrive when your world is breaking,*
*and they help you hold the pieces."*

For a brief time, it felt like Kanna had two sisters—one in silence, one in strength.

Aishu would message Keerthi, sharing little jokes:

"Hey stupid, your anna is not eating. Come scold him, please."

She even started calling them the "3AM Trio."

***"Because we're always up... you crying, me worrying, and Keerthi fighting for her life."***

They made an odd family, built not on blood, but on broken hearts, desperate love, and deep prayers.

October 30th – The Festival of Fire Without Light

Diwali was coming. The streets were being decorated. Firecrackers were sold at every turn. But in Kanna's world, it was all noise. Empty, echoing noise.

On October 30th, just one day before Diwali, another call came.

This time, there was no trembling voice. Just silence.

"Kanna... Keerthi's gone."

The Earth Fell Silent

Kanna dropped the phone.

His mother rushed in, asking what happened. But he couldn't speak. He just sat there, frozen. Tears didn't come immediately. They came later—like a tsunami after the earthquake.

He screamed into his blanket. Punched his pillow. Scratched at his chest like he could pull the pain out.

Keerthi...

The first person who called him "anna"...

The only sister who truly felt like home...

was gone.

*"She wasn't just a chapter in my story.
She was the only page that ever felt real."*

Aishu – The Light That Refused to Go Out
That night, Kanna didn't plan to sleep. Or eat. Or even live.
But Aishu called.
And called.
And called.
Until he finally answered.
She didn't speak at first. Just cried with him.
And then she said:
"If you leave too... who will keep Keerthi alive in memories?"
That sentence anchored Kanna. Not fully. Not permanently. But enough.
Days That Felt Like Dying in Slow Motion
In the weeks that followed, Aishu became his oxygen.
She stayed awake with him through panic attacks.
She distracted him with old songs.
She told him stupid jokes.
She listened to his pain.
When he said, "I don't want to live,"
she replied, "Then live for her."

*"Sometimes, one person doesn't just save your life...
They carry your soul through fire."*

Kanna started writing letters to Keerthi—unsent, but healing. Aishu encouraged it. She even wrote one herself and sent it to Kanna.

**"Dear Keerthi... you never knew, but your 'anna' is someone rare. Someone precious.
You should've stayed...
for him."**

A Family That Grief Built

By the end of the year, Aishu wasn't just a friend. She wasn't just a senior.

She was his sister.

Not a replacement for Keerthi.

But a different kind of miracle.

> *"Sometimes, the sky loses a star...*
> *But the universe gives you the moon to help you see again."*

# CHAPTER FOUR

# The Festival of Darkness

*""Some festivals are not about lights or sweets...*
*Sometimes, they're just painful reminders*
*of who didn't make it to this year's celebration."*

October 31st, 2020 – A Diwali That Never Came

The world was bursting in colors.

Fireworks danced in the skies. Homes glowed in fairy lights. Children laughed as they lit sparklers. Every corner of the city was alive.

Except Kanna's heart.
That night, it was darker than the blackest sky.

Keerthi had died just the day before. The girl who once joked about bursting crackers together, who painted Diwali cards for her classmates, was now lying in a hospital freezer, surrounded by silence.

Kanna sat in his room, staring at the ceiling. No lights. No lamps. No sounds of joy.

His mother had tried to lift the mood, unaware of the storm within him. She placed a few diyas on the windowsill, made his favorite sweets, and softly said:

"Light a diya for her soul, kanna. She'll see it from up there."
But Kanna didn't move.
Because how do you light a diya when everything inside you is already burned to ash?

*"Everyone else saw lights that night...*
*I only saw the shadow of someone who wasn't there."*

The Empty Corner of the Group Chat

In their old group chat—"Class 8B Stars"—Keerthi's profile still showed her bright, smiling face.

Nobody removed her.

No one had the heart to.

Aishu messaged there once:

"We miss you, Keerthi. This Diwali, the sky stole its brightest light."

Kanna read it. Typed something. Deleted it. Then just sent:

"You promised to stay forever, didn't you?"

The Cry That Woke the Walls

That night, around midnight, as the last of the fireworks faded into smoke and silence, Kanna broke.

He howled into the dark.

Fell to the floor.

Clutched his chest.

Whispered Keerthi's name over and over like a mantra.

He pulled out the rakhi she once tied him—still hidden inside his diary. Held it tight like it was the only thing keeping him on Earth.

His mother rushed in, frightened.

But Kanna couldn't explain the ache.

The kind of ache that didn't bleed.

Didn't bruise.

It just emptied.

"I didn't lose a friend.

I lost the one person who called me brother

like she meant it with her whole soul."

The next day, Aishu called. She had heard everything.

Her voice was calm but trembling.

"Kanna... if you break now, she'll disappear completely.

We have to keep her alive—in us."

She sent a voice note reading Keerthi's last message to her.

**_"Take care of kanna. He acts strong, but he's just a kid inside."_**
Kanna dropped the phone again.
That one message…
It shattered him.
And stitched him back, all at once.
15 Days of War
For two weeks, Kanna stopped eating properly.
Stopped talking.
Stopped responding to anyone except Aishu.
Aishu would call during meals, asking:
"Did you eat today?
Do you want me to scold you like Keerthi would?"
She even recorded herself singing old school songs—Keerthi's favorites. She read old chat screenshots like bedtime stories. She stayed up every night until Kanna fell asleep on the call.

*"When grief holds your throat,*
*you need someone who becomes your breath."*

Diwali Passed. But the Darkness Stayed.
People moved on. Festivals came and went.
But in Kanna's world, there was only before and after Keerthi.
Before her death, the world had color.
After her death, even the sun felt grey.
He started writing more letters. Long, unposted ones. All addressed to "Chelli."

*Excerpts from Kanna's Letters*
*"Keerthi… are you seeing me? I still remember how you scolded me for forgetting to eat lunch. Now I skip it every day, just to see if you'll come back to remind me."*
*"You called me 'anna' with more love than I ever thought I deserved. Now no one says it the same."*
*"I light a candle for you every night… but the flame never burns as bright as your smile."*

Aishu's Gift

One day, Aishu sent him a small handwritten poem she wrote, titled **"Sisters Never Die."**

> *""They become stars*
> *watching over their annas.*
> *They become wind*
> *whispering 'stay strong.'*
> *They become dreams*
> *that hug us in sleep.*
> *They become silence—*
> *the kind that still says,"*
> *'I'm here.'""*

Kanna cried for hours that night.

But for once, he didn't cry alone.

Diwali Season Ends. So Does a Chapter of His Life.

Aishu didn't let go.

Not once.

She wasn't just a sister figure now—she was the lifeline that held the shattered pieces of Kanna together.

But life, as always, was preparing for another cruel twist.

Because even the strongest bonds aren't safe from the world's judgment.

And the one light that helped Kanna survive... was slowly about to fade.

> *""The cruelest thing about grief*
> *is that the world moves on*
> *as if the person you lost*
> *was never here.""*

# The Second Goodbye

*" "Not all goodbyes come with closure.*
*Some just fade in silence,*
*leaving you wondering if you were ever needed at all." "*

A New City, A New Silence

Hyderabad was never meant to feel so far.

When Aishu left for her B.Tech after lockdown lifted, Kanna felt proud. She had worked hard. She deserved that future. He even helped her shortlist colleges, research hostels, and plan her move.

But no one tells you that sometimes...
the people you love don't leave with a bang.
They leave with a "brb" that never returns.

In the first few weeks, they stayed in touch—calls, voice notes, silly memes. She'd send him photos of her campus canteen, random pigeons on the window, and sleepy morning snaps.

He would smile at the screen and whisper,
"Don't forget me, chelli."
She never replied to that. She'd just send a red heart.
But red hearts can't stop time. And they can't stop fate either.
and soon....
Once, they spoke every hour.
Then it became every evening.
Then, every weekend.
Then... just festival wishes.

Kanna felt it before it happened.

The bond was slipping. Like sand in his hands.

He told himself:

"She must be busy. New life. New friends. It's okay."

But it wasn't okay.

Because Kanna wasn't asking for hours of her day.

He just wanted one minute—one minute to feel like he still mattered

March 2021. Holi.

Kanna had never really liked colors before. But this time, he planned to celebrate. Because Aishu was visiting her hometown for the holidays.

He thought:

"Maybe we'll meet. Maybe I'll finally hear her voice in person again."

He called her, full of excitement.

The phone rang.

And rang.

And then... she picked up.

But the voice on the other end?

It wasn't the same.

It was cold. Hesitant. Nervous.

"Kanna... please don't call me anymore."

His heart skipped.

"What happened, chelli?"

A long pause.

Then came the words that shattered everything:

"My parents... they saw our chats. They think I'm too close to you. They don't want me to talk to you anymore. They think... it's not right."

Kanna couldn't speak.

He held the phone in silence as his whole world went mute.

He wasn't angry.

He wasn't even surprised.

He was just... tired.

Tired of fighting for something that should've been simple—love without conditions. Siblinghood without blood. Connection without suspicion.

He whispered:

"So that's it? Just like that, I lose you?"

Aishu was crying on the other end.

But she didn't say sorry.

Because in her tears, Kanna heard what she couldn't speak aloud:

***"I want to stay. But the world won't let me."***

After the call ended, Kanna stared at the wall for hours.

His phone sat beside him, dead and cold.

Like the bond they once shared.

He didn't touch colors that Holi.

While the world painted each other with love, he drowned in the absence of it.

He took out the old audio messages Aishu once sent during Diwali.

***<u>"Smile for me, kanna… Keerthi would want you to smile."</u>***

He played it on loop. But this time, even those words couldn't save him.

Because this wasn't death.

This was abandonment.

And that hurts more. Because they're still alive. Still breathing. Just… choosing not to be there anymore.

***"You held me through my worst days.***

***But when the world questioned our bond,***

***you let go.***

***And that's the kind of silence that screams forever."***

" ✏? *The Diary Entry: "Another Sister, Another Scar"*

*"Dear Chelli Aishu,*

*I don't blame you. I blame the world that never understood us.*

*I know you loved me, even if the world told you not to.*

*But tonight, your silence is louder than all my cries.*

*You saved me once.*
*And now, I have to learn how to survive without you too.*
*Your anna, who never stopped waiting."*"*

Kanna removed Aishu's photo from his shelf.
Not out of anger.
But because looking at it hurt more than forgetting it.
He placed it inside a book—his silent graveyard of memories.
A place for the people who left without dying.
And just like that, the girl who once stood as his savior, his light, his support when Keerthi died... became just another name he whispered at night.
**Aishu—the second goodbye.**

*""I keep losing people.*
*Not to death.*
*But to the kind of silence that only the living can give."*"

# CHAPTER SIX

# Nisha – The Promise of Forever

*"Sometimes, the ones who promise to stay forever are the first to walk away... and never look back."*

After Aishu's goodbye, Kanna didn't cry.

He didn't scream, didn't punch walls, didn't even write.

He just... stopped feeling.

It was like someone had muted the world around him. Like he was a ghost walking through his own life.

Until she came.

Her name was Nisha—a sub-junior from his school.

It started with a simple text.

"Hi anna ☺? I heard about Keerthi akka and Aishu akka. I'm really sorry. You don't deserve this. I'm here if you need someone."

At first, he didn't reply.

He was tired of people who said they'd stay.

But she didn't give up.

Every morning:

"Good morning anna ♥?"

Every night:

"Sleep well anna... I'm always here ?"

There was no demand. No pressure. Just presence.

Slowly, unknowingly... Kanna started texting back.

? The Word He Had Forgotten: "Anna"

It had been months since someone called him "anna" with such warmth.

The way she said it—like she meant it.

*"Not just a title. Not just a formality.*
*But a bond. A belief. A promise."*

She would tell him about her school, her silly fights with friends, the teachers she hated.

He would laugh again—really laugh. Not the fake smile he wore for the world.

They started sharing songs. Voice notes. Inside jokes.

And one night, when she was crying about exam stress, Kanna stayed on call for hours, telling her stories until she fell asleep.

"You're the brother I prayed for, anna. Please don't leave me... ever."

Kanna's heart cracked open.

This... this was the sister he had waited for.

Her birthday was in December.

She hesitantly said,

"No one ever celebrated it properly before..."

So Kanna planned it like it was Diwali and Christmas and Raksha Bandhan in one.

He brought her cake. Balloons. Gifts she didn't expect. A tiny handwritten letter that said:

*"To my little sister,*
*You didn't walk into my life.*
*You filled the spaces left by those who walked out."*

That day, Nisha cried in his arms.

"No one has ever made me feel so loved, anna. I'll never forget this. I'll never leave you. Promise."

And Kanna believed her.

*""Some people don't give you memories.*
*They give you hope.*
*And when they leave, they don't just break your heart.*
*They destroy your belief in love itself.""*

And Then The Distance Begins Again

Kanna moved to Hyderabad for intermediate.

The college didn't allow phones. But every Sunday, he'd stand in line at the payphone just to hear her voice for 2 minutes.

"Annaaaa! I missed you. So much happened! Wait wait I'll tell everything!"

She would giggle, talk non-stop, ask about his health, even remind him to eat and drink water properly.

Those calls became his medicine.

Every day that felt like a burden, he carried through... just to reach Sunday.

He sent her letters through hostel friends. Drawings. Notes.

He made her feel loved.

And in return, she made him feel like family.

And then suddenly

One Sunday. Same line. Same routine.

He waited. Got the receiver.

But Nisha's voice... was different.

Cold. Distant.

"Anna... I have to tell you something."

"What happened, chelli?"

Long silence.

"I'm in a relationship. With a boy in my class. He doesn't like that I talk to you so much."

Kanna froze.

She continued—

"He saw our chats. Got jealous. He said he'll break up with me if I don't stop talking to you..."

"And what did you tell him?"

Her next words shattered him:

"I told him I'll stop.
Please anna... don't message or call me anymore."

*" "You promised forever.*
*But the moment he walked in,*
*you threw me out like I never meant anything." "*

on that day
He didn't cry on the phone.
He said, "Okay."
Just that.
One word.
A lifetime of silence behind it.
She never called again.
No birthday wishes. No check-ins. Nothing.
She erased him like he was a mistake.
Like all those "forevers" were just... noise.
And Kanna also deleted the chats.
But not before reading every message again—each "good morning anna," every "I love you anna," and all the "I'll never leave you" promises.
He sat alone in the hostel, holding the bracelet she gave him on her birthday.
It was pink, with a tiny charm that read "Brother".
He stared at it and whispered:

*" "Maybe I was never meant to be anyone's brother.*
*Maybe 'anna' is a word cursed in my mouth." "*

*" Diary Entry: "To the Girl Who Promised Forever"*
    *"Nisha,*
*I don't blame you. I blame the world that made you choose*
*between love and loyalty.*
*But did you really have to choose?*

*I celebrated your life like it was my own.*
*I protected your smile like it was sacred.*
*And now, you leave me for someone who can't even let you love your brother?*
*I hope he loves you well.*
*I hope you never feel the pain you gave me.*
*Just know... I meant every word.*
*Even if you never did."*

"It hurts, not because she left.
It hurts because she made me believe she never would."
And so, another bond ended.
Not in death.
Not in betrayal.
But in replacement.
She replaced him with a boy who couldn't understand sibling love.
And in doing so, she taught Kanna something brutal—

*"Forever is just a word people use until someone better comes along."*

# CHAPTER SEVEN

# The Word "Sister" Feels Like a Curse

*""Once, 'sister' felt like a blessing.*
*Now, it sounds like a lie wrapped in love, waiting to be*
*broken.""*

Nisha's goodbye wasn't loud.
There were no fights. No final "I hate you."
Just silence.
And in that silence, something inside Kanna snapped.
All the words he once used to write poems—gone.
All the hope he once poured into messages—dry.
All the colors in his world—turned to grey.
He didn't cry this time.
He didn't shout at the sky, or beg anyone to stay.
**Because what's the point of asking people to stay when every promise they make tastes like betrayal?**

*""I didn't lose my sisters.*
*I lost myself in the process of believing they were mine.""*

He started avoiding people.
He stopped replying to old friends. Stopped talking in class. Stopped looking in the mirror.

The only word that echoed in his head was:
"Why?"
Why did they leave? Why did they lie? Why did they come into his life just to walk away?
And worst of all...
Why did he still miss them?

> *"The pain doesn't come from their absence.*
> *It comes from how real their presence once felt."*

The pain was too much. Too constant.
It wasn't loud anymore—it was quiet.
The kind of pain that eats you alive in silence.
So Kanna tried something he never thought he would.
**He picked up a cigarette from a senior.**
It burned.
The smoke scratched his throat, made him cough like hell.
But for a moment...
Just one moment...
He felt nothing.
And "nothing" felt better than pain.
So he took another.
And another.
**Soon, smoking wasn't a mistake.**
**It was a ritual.**
His mind? Numb.
His heart? Hollow.
His soul? Tired.

> *"I didn't want to destroy myself.*
> *I just didn't know how else to survive without feeling anything."*

Someone once called him "anna" in college.
He walked away without replying.

The word now tasted like blood in his mouth.

It was cursed.

Every time someone said it, he remembered:

Keerthi's sudden distance, and her final silence

Aishu's goodbye on Holi, ordered by her parents

Nisha choosing her boyfriend over the bond she once said would never break

He didn't want another "sister."

Not again.

Not ever.

**_"'Anna' is not a word._**

**_It's a wound now."_**

One random evening, as Kanna sat alone on the college steps, smoke swirling around his face like a fog of his failures—

A text popped up on his phone.

"Hi Kanna... I know everything. I'm not here to hurt you. Just... listen?"

It was from Chinni, a classmate he barely noticed.

She had always been quiet in class. Not too talkative, not too bold. But she'd always observed from a distance.

And she had noticed him.

He didn't reply.

But she texted again the next day. And the day after.

"I know it's hard. But I also know you're not alone."

"You're stronger than this. Even if you don't believe it."

"One day, the pain won't hurt this much."

Her words weren't grand. But they were consistent.

She didn't ask him to stop smoking.

She didn't ask him to share everything.

She just... showed up.

> _"Sometimes, the loudest kind of love..._
> _is the quiet one that doesn't walk away."_

Weeks passed. Kanna hadn't smoked in two days.

He didn't know why. Maybe because every time he lit a cigarette, he remembered her words:

"You're stronger than this."

One night, she called.

He picked up.

"Kanna... are you okay?"

He didn't lie.

"No. I don't think I've been okay in years."

And for the first time in so long, he cried.

Not like a hero holding it in.

Not like a man swallowing his pain.

He cried like a boy who had been left too many times, loved too briefly, and hurt too deeply.

And Chinni... she just listened.

No judgments.

No advice.

Just presence.

*""Sometimes healing begins not with answers...*
*but with someone who doesn't walk away when you're broken.""*

From that day, Chinni started calling every evening.

Not to fix him. But to walk beside him through the ruins.

Kanna began laughing again—softly, at first.

He stopped smoking—one day at a time.

He started looking at the sunrise without wondering if he'd make it to sunset.

Not because the world changed.

But because someone finally stayed.

*""You don't need someone to save you.*
*You just need someone who won't run away when they see you drowning.""*

Kanna still flinched when someone said "sister."

But when Chinni started calling him anna... he didn't correct her.

Not this time.

Because maybe—just maybe—this bond wasn't here to break him.

Maybe this was the beginning of something new.

> *"You cannot erase the scars they left.*
> *But you can find someone who kisses the wounds and calls them beautiful."*

# CHAPTER EIGHT

# Chinni – The Tough Love

*""Sometimes love doesn't hug you softly.
Sometimes, it slaps the hell out of your habits until you wake
up from your self-destruction.""*

After weeks of small talks and daily calls, Chinni slowly became the only constant in Kanna's life.

She didn't act like a savior. She didn't try to erase the past.

She was just there—raw, real, and relentless.

Every night, she'd call after study hours.

"Finished revising?"

"Stop overthinking, just read page by page."

"Sleep, idiot. You need rest too."

She reminded him to drink water. To eat on time. To revise subjects he had long abandoned.

And Kanna? He didn't even realize when his grades started improving again.

He didn't realize when his eyes stopped looking hollow.

He didn't realize that for the first time in a long time—he was surviving without pretending.

"She didn't just heal my wounds.
She stood beside me when I didn't know I was bleeding."

Exam season hit hard.

The kind that drowns most students in anxiety.

But not Kanna—not this time.

Every night, Chinni would quiz him over the phone.

"Explain bioactive compounds, Mr. Kanna."

"Did you finish that organic chemistry chapter or were you scrolling Insta?"

He'd smile, hiding the grin in his voice.
"No ma'am. Finished twice."

Even her scoldings sounded like comfort.

Even her silence felt warmer than words.

> *"Some people walk into your mess like it's their home*
> *And clean it, piece by piece...*
> *Not because they have to—*
> *Because they want to."*

But good days have shadows.

And Kanna's shadows were still following him.

One day, between two exam sessions, stress mounted. He hadn't slept well, hadn't eaten, hadn't stopped thinking.

So he gave in.

One cigarette. One drag. One moment of weakness.

But one of Chinni's college juniors saw him outside the library, smoking behind a tea stall.

She didn't text him that night. She didn't call.

But the next day, she sent one simple message:

"Meet me after college. Park. No excuses."

Kanna arrived late.

Still half-confused. Still pretending like nothing was wrong.

He saw her standing under the tree, arms crossed, face unreadable.

She didn't smile.

She didn't greet him.

She walked straight up, looked him in the eyes, and slapped him.
Hard.

"What the hell is wrong with you?" she shouted, fists clenched.

"Do you want to die? After everything you've told me? After everything I stayed for? After the promises, after the tears—you think your pain gives you the right to destroy yourself?"

He stood frozen.

He'd been shouted at before.

He'd been left before.

But no one had ever hit him like they cared.

She didn't stop.

She snatched the cigarette box from his bag and smashed it to the ground.

Then picked up a thick stick from the bushes nearby and started hitting him—on his arms, legs, shoulders.

It wasn't random violence. It was anger coated in love.

Fury dressed as care.

"Every time you smoke, you burn a piece of me too.

And I'm done watching you disappear while I keep praying you'll stay."

She hit until her hands trembled.

Until her voice broke.

Until she dropped the stick and collapsed to the ground, crying like a little girl.

> *"Real love doesn't always look like peace.*
> *Sometimes, it looks like war—because they refuse to lose you."*

It started to rain.

Not heavy. Just a drizzle—like the sky itself was crying with them.

Kanna slowly kneeled down beside her, bruises fresh, but heart cracked open.

"Chinni..." he whispered.

"I promise... I swear... I'll never touch it again."

She looked up, face soaked with tears and rain.

"Don't promise me for me.
Promise me for the boy you were—before the world broke him.
For the boy who once dreamed.
For the boy who deserves to live without ashes in his lungs."
And right there, in the middle of an empty park, under the cloudy sky—
Kanna promised himself.
Not for Chinni.
Not for anyone else.
But for the version of him that still deserved peace.
"That day, I didn't lose a habit.
I gained a home in someone who wasn't scared to break me just to rebuild me."
But love that is loud... is also noticed.
Some villagers saw the park scene.
By evening, rumors spread like wildfire:
"A girl beating a boy in the park?"
"He was smoking? She was screaming?"
"What kind of relationship is this?"
And by nightfall, Chinni's father found out.
Next day, she was gone from college.
No text.
No goodbye.
Just vanished.
Kanna panicked. Called. Messaged. Cried.
Nothing.
Until, two days later, she finally texted back:
"I'm not allowed to attend anymore. They said you're a bad influence. They're shifting me."
Kanna didn't think twice.
He went straight to her house.
No fear. No shame. Just desperation.
He stood before her father, folded his hands.
And he told the whole truth.

Told him about the smoking.
Told him how Chinni saved him.
Told him how she slapped him not out of shame, but out of love.
"Uncle, your daughter didn't ruin me. She saved me.
If you take her away now, you're punishing her for doing the right thing."
It took time.
But somehow—maybe because of his sincerity, maybe because of the truth—her father finally agreed.
With conditions.
Chinni was allowed back.
But under supervision.
And they were not allowed to "be too close."
But that didn't matter.
They didn't need labels.
They just needed presence.

*"She didn't heal me because she had to.
She healed me because she couldn't bear to watch me bleed anymore."*

From that day forward, Kanna stopped smoking. Fully.
No cheating. No relapse.
Because every time he looked at a cigarette, he remembered her trembling hands... her broken voice... the fire in her eyes when she said:
"I will not lose you to ashes."
And he'd smile.
Because someone—at last—was willing to fight for him...
Even if it meant fighting him.

*"You showed me that even broken boys can be saved...
Not by softness alone,
But by a storm who refuses to let them drown."*

# CHAPTER NINE

# Dreams of Togetherness

*" "We didn't just plan a future...*
*We built a world.*
*But I never thought I'd be left in it alone."*

After the war they fought together—after the beatings, the promises, and the tears—Kanna and Chinni felt more than just close.

They felt... invincible.

Like no force in this world could pull them apart anymore.

They made a promise—not the kind made in passing, but the kind that echoed in hearts and hung in every shared silence.

"Let's stay together after Inter," Chinni said one evening, her voice soft under the moonlight.

"Even if we don't end up in the same college, at least in the same city... close enough to have coffee on weekends and study in the same library."

Kanna nodded.

He wasn't used to planning the future with someone.

But with her... he dared to.

"We didn't need a label.

We just needed a place in each other's tomorrow."

Kanna chose an engineering college—a decent one, near Chinni's dream institution.

He didn't care about fame or rankings.

All he cared about was proximity.

They were now ten minutes apart by bus.

One stretch of road away.

It felt like life was finally giving him back the pieces it stole.

Every weekend, they met at their favorite dosa stall.

She still bossed him around.

"Cut your nails, Anna."

"Drink more water."

"You look like a zombie, did you sleep at all?"

He'd smile.

She was the same Chinni—annoying, loving, loud, real.

They weren't siblings by blood.

But the connection was deeper than anything Kanna had ever felt.

He started smiling more.

He laughed louder.

He began living.

*""Not everyone who saves you stays.*

*But while she stayed, she made the world feel warm again.""*

Then... came the silence.

It started small.

First, it was a few delayed replies.

Then, no calls on weekends.

Then, excuses.

"Busy with internal exams."

"Had to help a friend."

"Just tired, Anna... not in the mood to talk."

Kanna didn't complain.

He thought maybe life had just caught up.

But it was more than that.

The warmth in her voice was missing.

Her words started sounding like they were wrapped in ice.

He kept trying.

Kept texting.

"You okay?"

"Did I do something wrong?"

"Tell me if you're hurt... please."

But silence has a cruelty of its own.

It answers you with absence.

*""Nothing breaks a heart more than watching the person who once held your pieces... slowly drop them one by one.""*

One afternoon, after several missed texts, Kanna couldn't hold it anymore.

He left his college campus, took a bus, and reached hers.

Waited outside the gate.

Eyes searching every passing face.

And then, he saw her.

She walked out with a group of friends—laughing.

Not the fake kind.

She was happy.

He called out, "Chinni!"

She stopped.

Her smile faded.

She walked toward him slowly.

"Anna... why are you here?" she asked flatly.

Kanna stammered, "I... I just... You weren't replying. I wanted to see you."

Her expression hardened.

"Kanna, we can't keep doing this."

His chest tightened. "Doing what?"

"This... this sibling drama. You are not the same. You've changed. And honestly... I don't feel that bond anymore."

"You're not my brother anymore."

The words hit harder than any slap.

Worse than betrayal.

Worse than death.

Because this wasn't someone leaving... this was someone erasing the relationship completely.

*"You can survive death.*

*But how do you survive someone choosing to un-love you?"*

Kanna stood frozen.

Thousands of memories screamed behind his eyes—the park, the exams, the dosa stall, the rainy promise.

And now?

All of it reduced to one cold sentence.

"You're not my brother anymore."

He didn't argue.

Didn't cry in front of her.

He simply nodded, turned, and walked away.

Each step felt like dragging a thousand knives through his chest.

And that night?

He didn't sleep.

He didn't cry.

He just... stared at the ceiling and wondered:

*"Was I really that easy to leave?"*

*"Am I cursed to lose every sister I dare to love?"*

"There's a special kind of heartbreak that comes

not from losing someone to death...

but from watching them choose life without you."

Every place in the city reminded him of her.

The library?

She once waited outside, scolding him for being late.

The tea stall?

She once made him drink bitter coffee just to make fun of his face.

The bus stop?

That's where she once hugged him tight and whispered,

"You're my forever anna."
Now?
All those places turned into graveyards.
Not of people.
But of memories.

*"She was my light...*
*But lights don't always burn out.*
*Sometimes, they just switch off and walk away."*

Kanna walked back to his hostel that evening—hollow, heavy, haunted.

He didn't tell anyone.

He couldn't.

Because how do you explain to someone that you lost someone who was still alive?

How do you grieve a goodbye that didn't even come with a reason?

This wasn't just another heartbreak.

This was proof.

Proof that no matter how much he gave...

No matter how deeply he cared...

He would always end up being the brother nobody kept.

*"They all called me 'Anna'...*
*But none of them stayed long enough to mean it."*

# CHAPTER TEN

# A Hollow Shell

*"They broke me so quietly,*
*That even my own heartbeat didn't notice*
*I was dying inside."*

After Chinni's sudden and cruel departure, something shifted permanently inside Kanna.

He didn't cry this time.

He didn't scream. He didn't beg.

He simply... shut down.

Like a switch had been flipped somewhere deep inside him.

No more texts.

No more late-night calls.

No more expectations.

He walked into his college every day like a ghost wearing a human skin.

His body was there... but Kanna, the boy who once laughed, once loved, once lit up rooms with his warmth—he was gone.

*"They didn't just leave.*
*They took parts of me with them."*

College moved on.

Friends joked, assignments were passed, exams came and went. But Kanna?

He sat in the last bench, head low, eyes empty, heart heavier than he could carry.

Sometimes, when a lecturer cracked a joke, the class would erupt in laughter.

But if you looked closely, Kanna would just... stare blankly.

Like the sound of joy had stopped reaching his ears.

People noticed.

They whispered.

"Wasn't he the guy who used to talk a lot?"

"Why does he always look so... lost?"

"I heard his sister left him or something."

But no one asked.

No one dared to touch the pain sitting in his silence.

Because sometimes...

the quietest people are carrying the loudest screams.

*""I wasn't just lonely.*
*I was surrounded by people*
*But still felt like I didn't exist.""*

Every night, when the hostel lights dimmed and the world slowly fell asleep...

Kanna's mind woke up.

Each ex-sister visited him like ghosts—Keerthi, Aishu, Nisha, Chinni.

Their laughter, their promises, their smiles—haunting instead of healing.

He didn't cry anymore.

He couldn't.

His eyes were dry. But his heart? Flooded.

And the worst part?

He started believing something terrible.

"Maybe I was never meant to be loved.

Maybe I was never enough for anyone to stay."

He stopped dressing well.

Stopped taking care of his health.

Some days, he didn't eat at all.

He became invisible, even to himself.

And yet—every time he walked past the mirror—he saw a stranger.

Not Kanna.

Not the boy who used to smile over a sister's message or wait hours just for a hug.

But a shell.

An echo.

A survivor of too many goodbyes.

"When you lose everyone who called you 'family'...

You stop calling yourself anything."

Then... one day... someone did notice.

A girl from his class. Quiet. Observant.

Her name?

Divya.

She had noticed Kanna for weeks.

The boy who always walked alone.

Who spoke to no one.

Who stared at his book but never turned a page.

And for reasons unknown... she walked up to him after class.

"Hey... you okay?"

It was such a simple question.

But it cracked something inside Kanna.

He didn't answer.

He just nodded.

And left.

But the next day, she sat beside him.

And the day after that... she offered him lunch.

And slowly... word by word, glance by glance...

Kanna started speaking again.

" *"Sometimes, it's not love that saves you.*

*Sometimes, it's just someone noticing you're still*

*breathing."*"

Divya didn't ask too many questions.
She didn't push him to talk about the past.
She just... showed up.
With coffee.
With assignments.
With silly jokes.
She reminded him of what it felt like to have someone in his corner.
Kanna didn't want to trust again.
But his heart?
It was too broken to fight the warmth.

  *"Healing doesn't always arrive like a storm.*
  *Sometimes, it tiptoes in wearing quiet eyes and kind hands."*

He started looking forward to class again.
He laughed—once.
It surprised even him.
He didn't call her "sister."
Not yet.
But the bond was growing.
And for the first time in a long time...
Kanna thought:
"Maybe... just maybe... this one won't leave."
But little did he know—
Sometimes, the sharpest knives come wrapped in comfort.

  *"Trust is not built in grand gestures.*
  *It's built in silence, in showing up, in staying.*
  *But betrayal?*
  *It wears the same smile... until it doesn't."*

# CHAPTER ELEVEN

# Divya – The Smile That Lied

*"*"The most painful kind of betrayal...
is not when your enemies hurt you,
but when the ones you trusted with your scars
turn them into weapons."*"*

Divya.

Her name itself felt like a pause in Kanna's storm.

She was soft-spoken. Curious. Calm. The kind of girl who didn't take space—she created it.

While Kanna was still mourning the graveyard in his chest, Divya became the flower that dared to grow there.

She would sit next to him, offer him her tiffin, share her notes.

Her laughter was gentle, never loud. But it was honest.

And for a boy who had forgotten what it meant to feel seen—she was the first light in a long, dark tunnel.

*"*"It wasn't love.
It wasn't obsession.
It was just peace—
And when you've lived in chaos,
even peace can feel like heaven."*"*

Divya started opening up too.

About her struggles. Her family. Her dreams.

They studied together. Ate together. Celebrated small moments. She once said, "I never had a brother... but if I did, I think it'd feel like this."

Kanna didn't reply.

But his silence spoke enough.

For the first time after years of loss and abandonment, Kanna started believing that this bond might actually last.

He began smiling again—genuinely.

He didn't feel the urge to isolate.

And when Divya called him "Kanna bro," it didn't trigger pain—it offered comfort.

*"Maybe I wasn't the brother nobody kept.*

*Maybe... I was just waiting for the right one to stay."*

Kanna had never been the type to hold back.

If someone meant something to him, he gave his all.

And with Divya, he did exactly that.

From buying her lunch every afternoon, to gifting her a phone case she admired in a shop window...

From organizing surprise birthday plans, to funding her short trips...

He didn't keep track of the money, or the hours, or the energy.

He didn't care.

**Because when someone gives you hope,**

**you don't pay attention to the cost—you're just grateful it exists.**

*"Some people give flowers.*

*Some give chocolates.*

*But I?*

*I gave people pieces of myself...*

*And they walked away carrying everything."*

Then... one day... Divya told him about a boy.

She hesitated, unsure. But Kanna had always been understanding.

So she opened up.

"There's a guy I like... but he's kinda aggressive. People say bad things about him. But I believe he's just misunderstood."

Kanna didn't judge.

Until he saw the guy.

Rough. Arrogant. Known for fights. Known for games.

Kanna felt the instinct again. The protective big brother inside him woke up.

"Divya... he doesn't seem like a safe person."

She brushed it off.

But Kanna couldn't.

And when he heard that the boy had hurt someone before, he gathered courage and told Divya everything.

Not to control her.

But to protect her.

To not fail another sister again.

"I didn't want to be the silent brother. I wanted to be the shield I never had."

One afternoon, after college...

Kanna got a call.

Unknown number.

He picked up.

"Hey... are you Kanna?"

"Yes."

"Come to the canteen lane. We need to talk. It's important."

He assumed it was about an assignment. A group project.

He walked down the narrow street behind the canteen.

Three boys were waiting.

One of them? The very boy Divya said she "liked."

Before Kanna could even process it—

A fist collided with his face.

Then another.

Then a kick to his ribs.
Three boys.
Against one broken-hearted soul.
They hit him.
They said words that made his soul burn.
"You think you can brainwash Divya against me?"
"Stay out of her life, loser."
"You're not her brother. You're just a burden."
His body hit the ground.
His mouth bled.
His vision blurred.
But his heart? That shattered all over again.
Because this wasn't just betrayal by fists—
It was betrayal by the very girl who smiled like peace.

*""You can forgive pain.*
*You can even forgive lies.*
*But how do you forgive someone...*
*who handed you to your enemies?""*

His friends rushed to the scene after a call.
They took him to the hospital.
Stitches. X-rays. Broken ribs. Concussion.
But no doctor could treat the emotional wound now wide open
in his chest.
While lying in bed, with saline dripping into his veins,
Kanna stared at the ceiling—
And remembered every bite of food he bought her.
Every little gift. Every protective warning.
Every time he smiled just because she existed.
And he cried.
Not from the pain of the beatings...
But from the pain of knowing—he was betrayed again.

*"Don't tell me to be strong.*
*Tell me how to survive when the ones I love*
*keep turning into monsters with my trust in their hands."*

The next morning...
His boys didn't sit quiet.
They marched to the other college.
They fought.
Not for revenge—but for justice.
The news spread. Police got involved. Complaints were made.
But what remained untouched... was Kanna's soul.
Because there is no complaint form for heartbreak.
No punishment for betrayal.
And no refund for love wasted.
After exams, Kanna went home.
He didn't return to college.
He couldn't.
Not with Divya's face haunting every corner of the campus.
Not with those memories clinging like shadows.
He looked at himself in the mirror.
Bruised face. Broken body.
But worst of all—
A heart that had no pieces left to break.

*"You keep calling it heartbreak,*
*but this wasn't my heart breaking...*
*This was my soul collapsing*
*under the weight of being left too many times."*

# CHAPTER TWELVE

# The Fall and the Fight

*" "Some battles are fought in silence.*
*Some wounds don't bleed.*
*But the loudest screams...*
*are the ones no one hears." "*

The antiseptic smell of the hospital had a way of making things feel unreal.

Beep. Beep. Beep. The heart monitor blinked steadily beside Kanna's bed.

His lips were cracked.

His cheek bruised.

One eye swollen.

His ribs ached with every breath.

But all of that... still hurt less than what lived behind his eyes.

The doctors stitched the wounds.

The saline kept dripping.

But no IV drip could restore a soul crushed by betrayal.

Kanna stared at the ceiling fan as if waiting for answers. Waiting for peace.

But all he got were memories.

Divya's laugh.

Her soft "anna" messages.

Her voice saying, "I'll always be there for you."

And the sharp echo of betrayal:

"You think you can stop me from loving who I want?"

"Stay away from Divya."

"You're just a problem, not her brother."

Each word was a knife twisting deeper.

*" "You're not supposed to beg someone*
*to treat you like a human.*
*But here I was, bleeding for a bond*
*that never truly existed." "*

Kanna hadn't even finished crying when his college friends stormed in.

Abhi, Sai, Manoj... his boys.

They didn't say much.

They didn't need to.

One look at his condition, and the fire in their eyes was louder than any scream.

**"Who did this?"**

**"Tell us their names."**

**"We'll make sure they never touch you again."**

Kanna tried to stop them.

Not because he didn't want justice.

But because he was tired of everything.

Tired of fights. Tired of trust. Tired of being hurt.

But Sai simply said:

"You kept quiet too many times.

This time, let us speak for you."

And they did.

The next morning, Kanna's friends showed up at the rival college.

They found the boys who attacked him.

There were no words exchanged.

Just fists. Just fury.

Just pain returning to the source it came from.

It wasn't about revenge.

It was about showing that Kanna wasn't alone anymore.

*"Some friendships don't ask questions.*
*They just pick up your broken pieces*
*and break the hands that shattered you."*

Kanna returned to college just in time for the semester exams.
His face still carried the evidence of what he'd endured.
But his eyes... they were colder now.
Divya tried to talk once.
He didn't respond.
She texted.
He blocked.
Because you don't talk to ghosts.
You mourn them.
You learn from them.
And then... you let them go.
The exam hall was suffocating.
Not because of the pressure—Kanna had dealt with worse.
But because every desk, every corridor, every bench... carried her scent, her voice, her betrayal.
He wrote his papers with a mechanical hand.
His brain was working.
But his soul had left the building long ago.

*"It's not that I failed to move on.*
*It's just that I was carrying graves instead of memories."*

On the last day of exams, after submitting his paper, Kanna walked out of the hall and stood still in the corridor.
The sunlight fell on his face, but it didn't warm him.
He took out his phone.
He opened his photo gallery.
Pictures with Divya.

Selfies. Group studies. Raksha Bandhan. Her smiling in new dresses he bought.

He stared at them.

One by one, he deleted everything.

And with each swipe, a part of him whispered:

"You didn't deserve this.

But you also don't deserve to carry it anymore."

Then he blocked her everywhere.

And that was it.

No closure. No goodbye.

Just silence.

And freedom.

> *"Sometimes healing isn't loud.*
> *It's just deleting the chat...*
> *and never checking the 'last seen' again."*

After exams, Kanna packed his things.

He didn't inform anyone.

No farewell selfies. No campus tour. No "goodbye" hugs.

He just left.

He stepped into the same house where he had cried for Keerthi...

where Aishu's voice once laughed on late-night calls...

where he first talked to Nisha and promised forever...

where Chinni's rakhi still lay in a drawer...

And now, he returned once again.

Not as a boy hoping for a sister.

But as a young man who had lost every one of them.

His mother opened the door and gasped.

"What happened to your face, kanna?"

He hugged her tightly.

Fell to the floor.

And wept.

Not just for Divya.

But for every goodbye that was never really spoken.

*""I've seen girls tie rakhis with smiles.*
*But I've also seen those threads*
*turn into nooses around my hope.""*

For weeks, Kanna barely spoke.
He stayed in his room.
The lights remained off even during the day.
He ate in silence.
He avoided old friends.
He ignored every ping, every notification.
There was no dramatic ending.
Just... a slow, suffocating silence.
The kind where your heart beats, but you wish it didn't.
The kind where you're not dying... but you're not living either.

*""Some people survive heartbreak.*
*Others survive themselves afterward.*
*I was trying to do both.""*

# CHAPTER THIRTEEN

# Walking Away

*""Some endings don't need doors slamming.*
*Sometimes, it's just the sound of your footsteps...*
*walking away from everything you once begged to stay.""*

The second year of college had barely begun, but for Kanna...
it already felt over.

He sat alone in the campus canteen, staring at his untouched chai.

Groups of students passed by laughing, shouting, making memories.

Kanna?

He was a ghost walking through those halls—seen, but never really there.

He watched people smile with ease, something he hadn't done in months.

No more Keerthi.

No more Aishu.

No more Nisha.

No more Chinni.

And now... even Divya had turned into another scar.

*""When you bury too many bonds,*
*even the sky starts feeling heavier.""*

One evening, Kanna looked at the mirror in his hostel room.
His face was thinner.
His eyes had lost their shine.
Even his reflection looked like it wanted to escape.
That night, without telling anyone, he packed his bag.
Not just clothes—but the weight of everything he had carried for too long.
He dropped out.
Not because he couldn't pass.
But because he couldn't breathe.

*"People say don't quit.*
*But what if quitting*
*is the only way to survive?"*

His mother opened the gate, surprised.
"Kanna? You didn't tell me you were coming."
He didn't answer.
She noticed the exhaustion in his shoulders—the kind of tiredness that no sleep could fix.
She didn't ask further.
She just hugged him tight.
That hug—was the warmest thing Kanna had felt in months.
And the moment he stepped inside, he dropped everything.
Back in his childhood room.
Same old fan.
Same bed.
Same posters.
But he was different.
Emotionally hollow.
Spiritually drained.
Kanna had returned to the place he started...
but not as the boy who left.

*"*"Coming home felt like coming back to my grave.*
*I didn't live here anymore.*
*I just came to rest in peace."*"

Days passed.

Kanna barely left his room.

He would lie down for hours, not sleeping, not thinking—just existing.

Sometimes he'd scroll through his old photos.

Rakhi selfies.

Birthday cakes.

Long chats that ended with "I'll never leave you."

He tried deleting them.

But every time he hovered over "Delete," something stopped him.

Maybe because those memories were the only proof that those bonds were once real.

Even if they ended...

he needed to believe they had existed.

He would replay conversations in his mind like broken cassettes:

**"Anna, you're the best thing that happened to me."**

**"I'll never leave you, I promise."**

**"Please don't cry, I'm always here."**

**"You've changed. I don't need you anymore."**

The contrast...

was killing him.

*"*"Memories don't knock.*
*They break in,*
*every time you think you've finally healed."*"

His mother tried to talk.

She asked gently, cooked his favorite dishes, sat beside him in silence.

But Kanna didn't respond much.

"Eat this, kanna."
"You haven't gone outside in days."
"Please say something."
He would just nod. Or say "Hmm."
His voice... had gone into hiding.
And his heart had forgotten how to trust.
No more replies.
No more expectations.
Just... quiet.
His WhatsApp still had messages.
Some college mates.
Some juniors.
Even a few "Happy Rakhi" texts from random numbers.
He didn't reply to any.
He had nothing left to give.

*""The worst part about being broken
is that even love starts to feel like a threat.""*

Every night, sleep would pretend to come.
But as soon as he closed his eyes, the nightmares began.
Not of monsters or ghosts.
But of moments.
Keerthi's eyes when she first called him "Anna"
Aishu's last Holi message.
Nisha's birthday promise.
Chinni beating him with tears in her eyes.
Divya laughing... then turning away while he bled.
Each memory, sharp as glass.
And Kanna?
He walked barefoot through them every night.
He often whispered to himself:
"What did I do wrong?"
"Why did they all leave?"
"Why am I never enough to be kept?"

There were no answers.
Only echoes.

> *"They say time heals.*
> *But what if time is just another name for silence?"*

One day, while cleaning his cupboard, he found an old diary.
It was from 9th grade.
The year Keerthi entered his life.
He opened a random page:
**"Keerthi told me I'm like the brother she never had.**
**I smiled all night. I feel like I finally belong somewhere."**
He turned another page:
**"Aishu texted today. She said she'll protect me.**
**Two sisters in my life now. Is this what happiness feels like?"**
Another page:
**"Chinni said she'll join a college near mine.**
**We'll never drift. That's a promise."**
Kanna couldn't read anymore.
He shut the book and pressed it to his chest.
Tears fell like monsoon rain.
Silent. Relentless. Cleansing.
But they didn't wash away the pain.
They simply reminded him he could still feel.

> *"You know you're healing*
> *when your tears no longer surprise you."*

Weeks passed.
One evening, Kanna walked to the terrace.
The sky was painted in shades of orange and purple.
He stood there, wind brushing his face, watching people walk home.
A little girl passed below, holding her brother's hand.
He smiled at her.

She smiled back.

And that moment...

didn't hurt.

For the first time in a long time... it didn't hurt.

That night, Kanna wrote in his own diary:

> *"I think I've stopped expecting.*
> *I'm not waiting for anyone to come back.*
> *Not hoping for a 'sorry' or a 'miss you.'*
> *I'm learning to live in the space they left behind."*
> *"Maybe I'm not the brother they needed.*
> *But I was the brother they had.*
> *And I gave them everything."*

Kanna didn't fully heal that month.

Healing isn't a straight road—it's a spiral.

You revisit pain, again and again, each time with a little more strength.

But he was walking now.

Not running.

Not hiding.

Just... walking.

Away from pain.

Away from false promises.

Toward peace—even if it was far away.

And that's how Chapter 13 ends.

With Kanna walking—not to forget.

But to finally remember who he was before the heartbreak.

> *"I was the brother nobody kept.*
> *But I kept every one of them.*
> *In prayers.*
> *In memories.*
> *In scars."*

The soft hum of the ceiling fan above did nothing to silence the storm within Kanna. The screen of his phone glowed beside him, casting harsh light on his tired face. There it was—a ghost from the past, resurrected through a new Instagram ID.

"Hello Anna♥? I miss you ?"

The words.

Her words.

Divya's.

Kanna sat there like stone—eyes red, heart screaming silently.

"I just want to express my feelings..."

She poured paragraph after paragraph—blaming her anger, misunderstanding his possessiveness, saying she didn't realize his worth until he was gone. She missed him. She missed the bond.
She wanted to fix it.

But how do you fix a soul that was already burned to ash?

The Kanna reading the message wasn't the same boy who once waited for her call, who skipped meals just to hear her laugh, who defended her like a brother would—even when it meant facing fists alone.

That boy... was buried.

And this—this apology—felt like someone laying flowers on a grave they helped dig.

"Let's fix this..."

Kanna read those final three words over and over, then slowly closed the chat.

He didn't reply. He didn't block.
He simply opened a blank page in his diary.

# CHAPTER FOURTEEN

# Letters to the Sisters Who Left

"*To Keerthi — My First Sister*
*"You were the first to call me 'anna' and mean it. You taught*
*me what it feels like to be loved unconditionally... until you*
*didn't survive your pain. I still remember the last time we*
*laughed. I never thought that would be the last time."*

**"Not all goodbyes come with warning signs. Some just... end you."**

"*To Aishu — My Festival of Laughter*
*"We fought with colors on Holi, but my life turned grey when*
*your parents drew a line between us. I still check my phone*
*during every festival... hoping for a 'Happy Holi Anna' that*
*never comes."*

**"Love doesn't always die in storms. Sometimes it fades in silence."**

"*To Nisha — My Forever That Never Was*
*"You were my home in a world that didn't feel like mine. I*
*was your 'anna' until your boyfriend told you not to call me*
*that anymore. And you listened. I wish I mattered even half*

*as much as he did to you."* **"**

"Don't promise someone forever if you plan to leave by the weekend."

**"***To Chinni — My Discipline and My Disaster*
*"You slapped the cigarette out of my hand and called me your responsibility. But when rumors rose, and I stood alone... you walked away without a second thought. I wonder, did I ever mean anything beyond your image?"* **"**

"Some people only stand by you when the world is clapping, not when it's pointing fingers."

**"***To Divya — The Smile That Lied*
*"You smiled while I bled. You called me brother and still sent strangers to beat me. But when your texts returned, full of apologies and love, my heart didn't leap. It broke again — this time, quietly. Because I finally understood... your love came with a price tag. My peace."* **"**

"The cruelest lies are wrapped in words like 'I miss you' and 'Let's fix this.'"
Kanna finishes the last letter, tears staining the paper.
He doesn't send them.
He just folds them all and places them in an envelope labeled:

**"To the Sisters Who Taught Me Love, and Left Me With Lessons."**
And then — silence.

*"They called me Anna. They gave me names, festivals, dreams... and then they left. But I kept every memory — not because I'm weak, but because I once loved without asking for anything back."*

And the next Day kanna went to the park with the letter he written

The orange sunset bled into the broken benches of the old park — the same one where Kanna and Keerthi once sat, sharing dreams, candy, and laughter.

Kanna walked slowly across the cracked pathway, a small letter trembling in his hands.
The air smelled of rain, as if the sky was holding back tears just like him.

Kanna's tought:
"You were the first to call me 'Anna'... and the first to teach me what irreversible loss feels like."

He sat on the same bench where Keerthi once tied a friendship band around his wrist, saying,
"From now, you're my real brother."

He unfolded the letter and began reading aloud, as if she were sitting beside him.

"Dear Keerthi,
I don't know where to start.
You were my first definition of family outside blood.
You called me 'Anna' with a smile so pure that even the world's cruelty couldn't touch it.
You held my hand through my loneliest birthdays. You fought for me like a lioness.
You taught me what sisterhood meant.

And then... you left. Not by choice.
Life snatched you away before I even knew how much you meant.
I still remember the call... the way my legs gave out... the way my world blacked out.
I wasn't ready.
I am still not ready.

I kept thinking — maybe if I had called you that night, maybe if I had noticed your silence, maybe if I had hugged you tighter the last time we met... maybe you'd still be here.

I'm sorry, Keerthi.

I'm sorry I wasn't the brother you needed when you were fighting battles alone.

I know you wouldn't want me to blame myself.

I know you'd punch my shoulder and say, 'Anna! Don't overthink!' But your absence is louder than any advice.

I miss you.

I miss you in the spaces between every fake smile.

I miss you when festivals come and your name isn't the first wish I get.

I miss you... every time I call someone 'sister' and hesitate, terrified of losing again.

I hope wherever you are, you're smiling, teasing me, calling me 'dumbo' like old times.

I love you, Keerthi.

Always.

Your forever Anna,

Kanna."**

Kanna folded the letter carefully and placed it on the bench.

A small breeze lifted the letter slightly — almost like someone reaching out to touch it.

And for a brief moment...

Kanna smiled through his tears.

Because somewhere deep in his heart, he knew...

Keerthi never really left.

She just became a part of the air, the sunsets, and the strength he carried on days he thought he couldn't move forward.

"

*"Some goodbyes are permanent.*

*But so is the love they leave behind."*"

# CHAPTER FIFTEEN

# The Brother Nobody Kept

"Maybe I was the brother nobody kept, but I still kept every one of you in my heart."

The sun had started rising over the town where Kanna was born—a new day, a new beginning. But for Kanna, it felt like both an ending and a rebirth.

He stood silently at the edge of his rooftop, watching the morning sky slowly bleed from blue to orange. His fingers trembled, holding a small paper—one last letter he had written the night before. His eyes were swollen, his heart heavier than ever, but for the first time in years... he wasn't numb.

This was not the same boy who had once searched every girl's affection for a sister's warmth.

This was not the same Kanna who begged people to stay.

This was not the same boy who spent sleepless nights replaying broken promises.

No.

This Kanna was burnt, scarred, shattered—but still standing.

"Maybe I was always meant to be the one left behind," he whispered, as tears clung to the corners of his eyes.

He opened his drawer—inside it were six envelopes.

Each one holding a piece of his soul.

Letters never sent. Words never spoken. Pain never expressed.

He picked them one by one, placed them in a small box, and locked it with a trembling hand.

Then he looked at himself in the mirror.

For the first time in five years... he looked straight into his own eyes without shame.

A Promise Rekindled

Later that evening, Kanna visited a law college.

His steps were slow, hesitant—but determined.

Keerthi's old dream—the one she talked about during their very first call—echoed in his mind.

**"Anna... nenu lawyer avvali. Naa goal avnu nenu lawyer avvadam..."**

That dream had died with her... but a part of him still believed it deserved to live.

So he walked into the admission office.

No certificates in hand. No formal attire. Just a boy with a broken heart, and a fire lit by love.

"I want to study law," he told the clerk. "Not just for me... but for someone who believed in justice more than anything."

As he stepped out of the college, the sun had set. It was dark and a bit cold.

On the road nearby, a little girl—barely ten—was crying beside her cycle, which had a flat tire. No one stopped.

Kanna did.

He walked up to her and smiled softly.

"Hey, what happened?"

"I fell. Everyone went home. Amma will scold me," she sobbed.

He helped her stand, checked the cycle, and carried it on his shoulder as he walked with her for 2 kilometers.

The girl kept talking, like a little bird chirping in spring.

Kanna just smiled.

And for the first time... he didn't cry when someone called him "Anna."

He just let the word pass through him—not like a stab, but like a breeze.

That night, he sat down to write.

Not another letter. Not another goodbye.

But a truth.

*""Maybe I was the brother nobody kept.*
*Maybe I wasn't strong enough.*
*Maybe I gave too much.*
*Maybe I wanted too little.*
*But in every broken promise, in every unanswered call, in every betrayal—*
*I still chose love.*
*And I still kept every one of you in my heart.""*

He looked up at the sky.
One star. Then two. Then a dozen.
He smiled, whispering into the night.

*""Keerthi... I'll fight for justice, like you wanted.*
*Aishu... I'll protect bonds, like you taught me.*
*Nisha... I'll forgive, even when it hurts.*
*Chinni... I'll stay strong, even when no one believes in me.*
*Divya... I'll walk away from what breaks me.*
*And to all of you...*
*I'll carry you in every beat of my heart.""*

As dawn approached again, Kanna opened his window.
The wind was soft. The world was quiet.
Inside, there was still pain... but it no longer felt like a curse.
Because somewhere deep down... healing had begun.
He didn't know what tomorrow held.
He didn't know if anyone would ever stay.
But he knew one thing—
He was the brother nobody kept.
But he... never let go.
And that—was his greatest strength.
**"To the world, I may be no one.**
**But to the ones I loved... I was someone.**
**And that's enough for me."**
**<u>– The Brother Nobody Kept</u>**

# For Every Broken Soul Who Still Chooses Love

To the reader holding this book in trembling hands,
To the one wiping tears quietly while no one is watching,
To the soul who has been left again and again and again…
This is for you.
Maybe you were like Kanna.
Maybe you gave too much, cared too deeply, expected too little but still ended up shattered.
Maybe all you ever wanted was a "Are you okay?", but got silence.
Maybe you carried people in your heart who didn't even remember your birthday.
Maybe you were the one who stayed up crying while they slept peacefully.
Maybe you were the "brother nobody kept."
But you know what?
You are still here.
Breathing.
Healing.
Loving.
And that… is nothing less than a miracle.
Because even after the betrayals,
Even after the heartbreaks,
Even after the people you would've died for left you without a word—
You still choose love.
You still smile at strangers.
You still check in on your friends.
You still believe in soft hugs, late-night talks, and forever bonds.
That makes you rare.
That makes you beautiful.
That makes you unforgettable.
So here's to you—

The silent warrior.
The abandoned soul.
The forgotten sibling.
The one who never gave up.
You are not alone.
And maybe... just maybe...
One day, someone will look at you and say—
"Where were you all my life?"
And you'll smile and whisper...
"Waiting. Still loving. Still healing."
Forever and always,
With all my heart,


– Kanna
The Brother Nobody Kept

www.ingramcontent.com/pod-product-compliance
Lightning Source LLC
Chambersburg PA
CBHW020457160726
47991CB00007B/2703